TORTOISE
VS
HARE
THE REMATCH!

Written by
Preston Rutt

Illustrated by
Ben Redlich

START

Good evening sports fans, I'm Jonny Fox. Welcome to Race Night Live! You join me this Saturday night from the Tree House, for the build-up to the most exciting race of the year. It's the big one. **It's Tortoise vs Hare**

The Rematch.

In red we have our challenger.
Former champion, land speed record holder,
the fastest fur in the forest,
Harry 'The Hurricane' Hare!!!

Hare

Age:	5
Style:	Fast and furious
Wins:	81
Losses:	1
Favourite Food:	Fast food

In blue we have the athlete who caused
one of the biggest sporting upsets in history.
It's the one, the only, the defending champion of the wood,
'Steady' Eddie Tortoise!!!

Tortoise

Age: 61

Style: Easy does it

Wins: 1

Losses: 0

Favourite   Slow-roasted
Food: tomatoes

Let's look back at an absolutely astounding week:
On Monday our runners arrived and WOW,

what a scorcher!

The sun was **so hot** that
Tortoise didn't train at all!

Hare shadowboxed all day long
in the burning heat. And boy
was he **strong as an ox!**

On Tuesday we woke up to a **wicked, westerly wind!**

It was **so blustery** that Tortoise didn't train at all!

Hare chased leaves in the ghastly gale. And boy was he **fast as a cheetah!**

On Wednesday it rained **cats and dogs!** The downpour was **so dreadful** that Tortoise didn't train at all! Hare swam widths of the wide, wild river. And boy was he **menacing as a shark!**

On Thursday the hail
hammered down!
The hailstones were **so huge**
that Tortoise didn't train
at all! Hare played golf with
the humongous balls of ice.
And boy was he **powerful**
as a tiger!

On Friday it **blew a blizzard!**
The wind was so wild, the air so cold and the snow
so thick that Tortoise didn't train... **at all!**
Hare trained harder than ever.

He raced, chased, **swam...**
and ran!

And boy was he
fit as an arctic fox!

Now it's Saturday night.

It's time. Time to stop the chat and start the stopwatches. Time to learn who's the champ and who's the chump. Time for

Tortoise vs Hare
The Rematch
to begin!!!

Over to you, Cat Freeman, at trackside.

Cat Freeman: Thanks Jonny,
I'm here with Hare and Tortoise.
Hare, you've been training hard,
can you win back your crown?

Hare: *I'm good.*
Just too good for the wood.
I'm gonna make Tortoise look
like a Christmas pud.
There's only one runner should
rule this neighbourhood.
Understood?

Cat Freeman: Er...
thank you, Hare. Tortoise,
what do you say to that?

Tortoise: W–e–l–l...

Cat Freeman: Sorry,
Tortoise, I'll have to
stop you there. The race
is about to start.
Back to the studio!

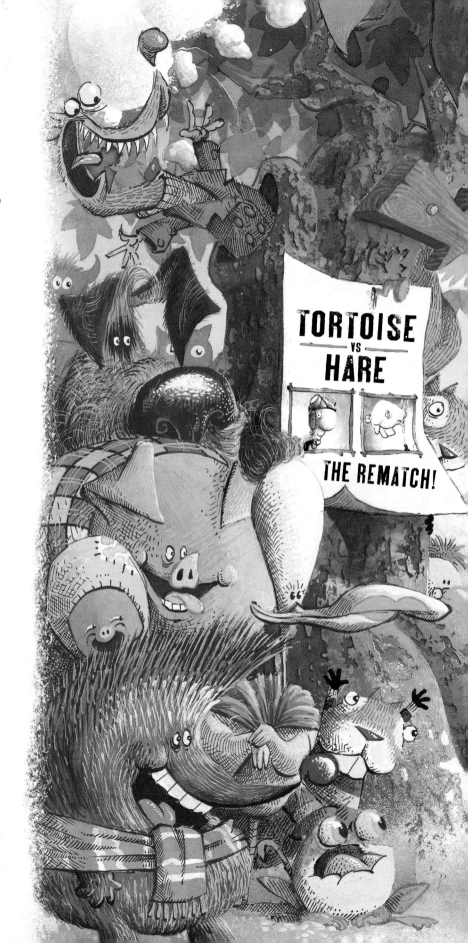

TORTOISE
VS
HARE

THE REMATCH!

And Tortoise is finally, ahem, into his...

...stride.

Whoops...

...a...

...daisy!

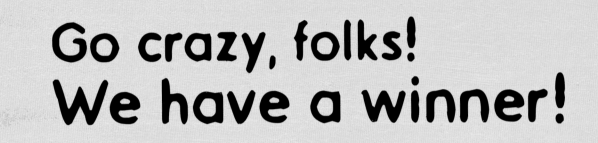

Go crazy, folks!
We have a winner!

Ahem,
I said good night!

Excitement over.
Close your eyes now
please! Thank you.
Good night.

For Mum & Dad,
my champions

P.G.R.

For Jasmine
& Asher

B.R.

Tortoise Vs. Hare
Text Copyright I Preston Rutt
Illustration Copyright I Ben Redlich
The rights of Preston Rutt and Ben Redlich to be
have been asserted by them in accordance
with the Copyright, Designs and Patents Act, 1988

Published by Hutton Grove,
an imprint of Bravo Ltd., in 2015
Sales and Enquiries:
Kuperard Publishers & Distributors
59 Hutton Grove, London, N12 8DS, United Kingdom
Tel: +44 (0)208 446 2440
Fax: +44 (0)208 446 2441
sales@kuperard.co.uk
www.kuperard.co.uk

Published by arrangement with Albury Books,
Albury Court, Albury, Oxfordshire, OX9 2LP.

ISBN 978-1-857338-14-0 (paperback)

A CIP catalogue record for this book
is available from the British Library
10 9 8 7 6 5 4 3
Printed in China